A tale of Moominvalley

PUFFIN BOOKS

UK | USA | Canada | Ireland | Australia | India | New Zealand | South Africa

Puffin Books is part of the Penguin Random House group of companies
whose addresses can be found at global.penguinrandomhouse.com.

www.penguin.co.uk   www.puffin.co.uk   www.ladybird.co.uk

Penguin
Random House
UK

First published 2019
001

Characters and artwork are the original creation of Tove Jansson
Written by Richard Dungworth
Text and illustrations copyright © Moomin Characters™, 2019
All rights reserved

Printed in China
A CIP catalogue record for this book is available from the British Library

HB: 978-0-241-37619-5
PB: 978-0-241-37620-1

All correspondence to:
Puffin Books, Penguin Random House Children's
80 Strand, London WC2R 0RL

MOOMIN

and the

Golden Leaf

BASED ON THE ORIGINAL STORIES BY

Tove Jansson

PUFFIN

In Moominvalley, the coolness of autumn was in the air. Moomintroll was out picking the last of the wild berries for Moominmamma's forest fruit punch. It was the Autumn Ball that night, and all the valley folk would be there.

"Do you think there'll be fireworks?" squeaked Sniff.

"I expect so," said Moomin, trying to sound excited. The day before, his best friend, Snufkin, had headed off on his travels. Moomin missed him already.

"Pee-hoo!" he sighed to himself.

"Moomintroll! Look!"
Sniff was pointing at the forest floor, his eyes wide. Something there glittered with the gleam of –

"Gold!" squeaked Sniff.

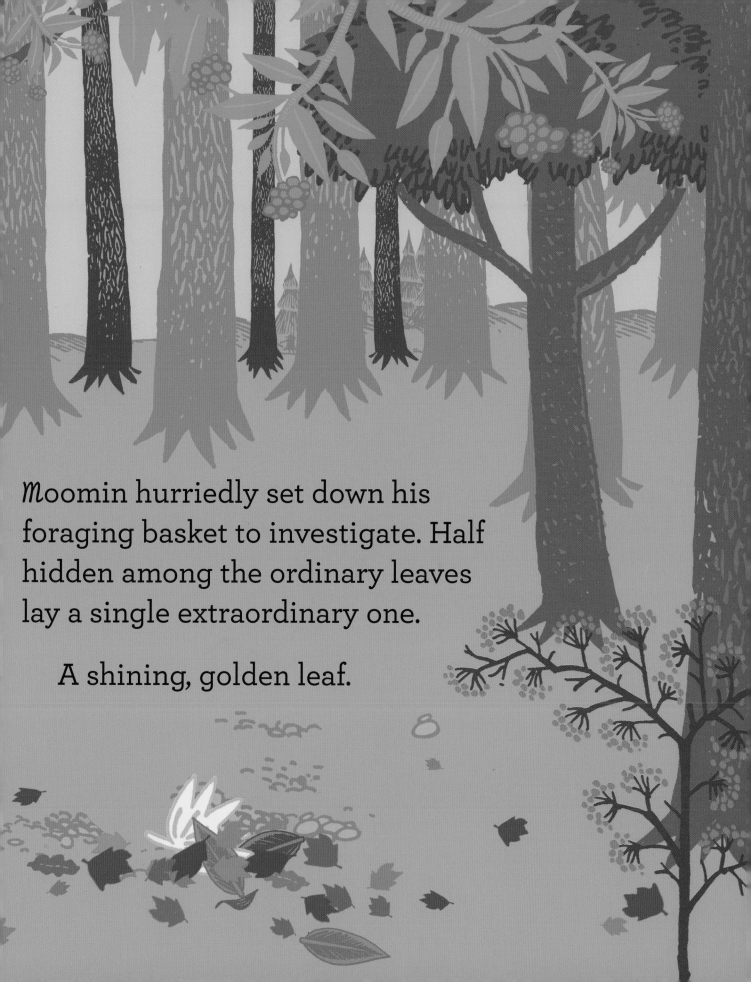

Moomin hurriedly set down his foraging basket to investigate. Half hidden among the ordinary leaves lay a single extraordinary one.

A shining, golden leaf.

Sniff and Moomin gazed at their marvellous discovery.

"This must be from a tree full of golden leaves!" squeaked Sniff. "We have to find it right away!" His whiskers drooped as he gazed at the forest all around him. "But how?"

Moomintroll felt giddy. If they could find that tree, he would be able to give a leaf to everyone at the Autumn Ball! It made him smile to think how happy the valley folk would be.

Moomin picked a tree with branches low enough to reach and began to climb.

The climb was far from easy, but it was worth it. When he got to the top, Moomintroll could see out across the whole forest.

In the wide, whispering sea of treetops,
there were leaves of many different colours –
greens, yellows, oranges and rusty browns.

But Moomin couldn't spy a tree
with golden leaves anywhere.

Climbing down proved
even trickier than
climbing up. The breeze
made the tall tree sway.

Moomin looked for
the ground and felt
his tummy turn.

He was taking a short rest to recover his courage when a shrill scream split the air.

Moomin gasped. "Snorkmaiden!"

Moomin clambered down the remaining branches as quickly as he could.

"It came from over here!" cried Moomin, dashing through the trees to Snorkmaiden's rescue.

Sniff, who considered himself rather too small to be brave, scampered behind.

"What if it's outlaws?" he squeaked. "Or robbers?"

It wasn't outlaws or robbers. In a clearing, they found Snorkmaiden with Moominpappa, Little My, and Too-Ticky. All four were dressed up.

Sniff's eyes fixed on the golden wreath perched on Moominpappa's ears.

"We're rehearsing a surprise performance," Moominpappa explained. "For tonight. I wrote the story myself. I call it *The Emperor and the Ant-Lion*."

"I'm the Ant-Lion!" declared Little My proudly. "Raarrrr!" she growled.
"And I'm a damsel in distress," said Snorkmaiden. "There's lots of screaming to get right!"

The Emperor and the Ant-Lion

$\mathcal{S}$niff looked from the leaf in his paw to Moominpappa's head.

"It must have fallen off that," he said, a little sadly. "Not from a golden tree. It's just painted gold."

Sniff looked crestfallen. Moomin sighed. There was no golden tree! Now he wouldn't be able to give any gifts at all.

Sniff's disappointment quickly passed when
Moominpappa offered to add him to his story –
as the Emperor's Guard.

"And you can take my place as the hero,"
Too-Ticky told Moomin. "I'd much rather have
a non-speaking part."

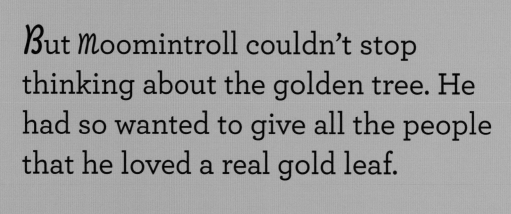

But Moomintroll couldn't stop thinking about the golden tree. He had so wanted to give all the people that he loved a real gold leaf.

"Moominmamma, Moominpappa, Little My, Snorkmaiden. And when Snufkin comes back . . ." he murmured, "what would Snufkin do with his?"

Moomin shrugged. Snufkin didn't care much for things.

"Ahem!" Moominpappa coughed loudly. "No time for day-dreaming, Moomintroll. We've got to practise our parts. The Autumn Ball will be starting before you know it!"

Moominpappa was right. In no time at all the performance of *The Emperor and the Ant-Lion* was ready to begin.

The show was a triumph. Moomin looked out at all the happy, smiling faces and his heart flushed with pride. "Bravo! Bravo!" cheered the valley folk, as the actors took their bows.

After the performance, there was dancing, feasting and fireworks. Moominmamma had created a magnificent spread from the autumn harvest.

Moominpappa cleared his throat to make a toast. "Ahem! To family ... To splendid neighbours ..."

He caught Moomintroll's eye. "And to absent friends."

"To friends everywhere," agreed Moomintroll, raising his glass, "for making me richer than my wildest dreams."

Moomin looked up at the bright stars in the clear autumn sky. The same stars would be twinkling down on Snufkin, too.

"Goodnight, Snufkin," whispered Moomintroll, with a smile.

Then he closed his eyes, and remembered all of the magical times they had shared together. Each memory was a treasure, more precious than any gift he could have given. He drifted off into a sweet dream about his friend – beneath a beautiful tree with leaves all of gold.

The End